BOTS

ADVENTURES OF THE SUPER ZEROES

by Russ Bolts

illustrated by Jay Cooper

LITTLE SIMON
New York London Toronto Sydney New Delhi

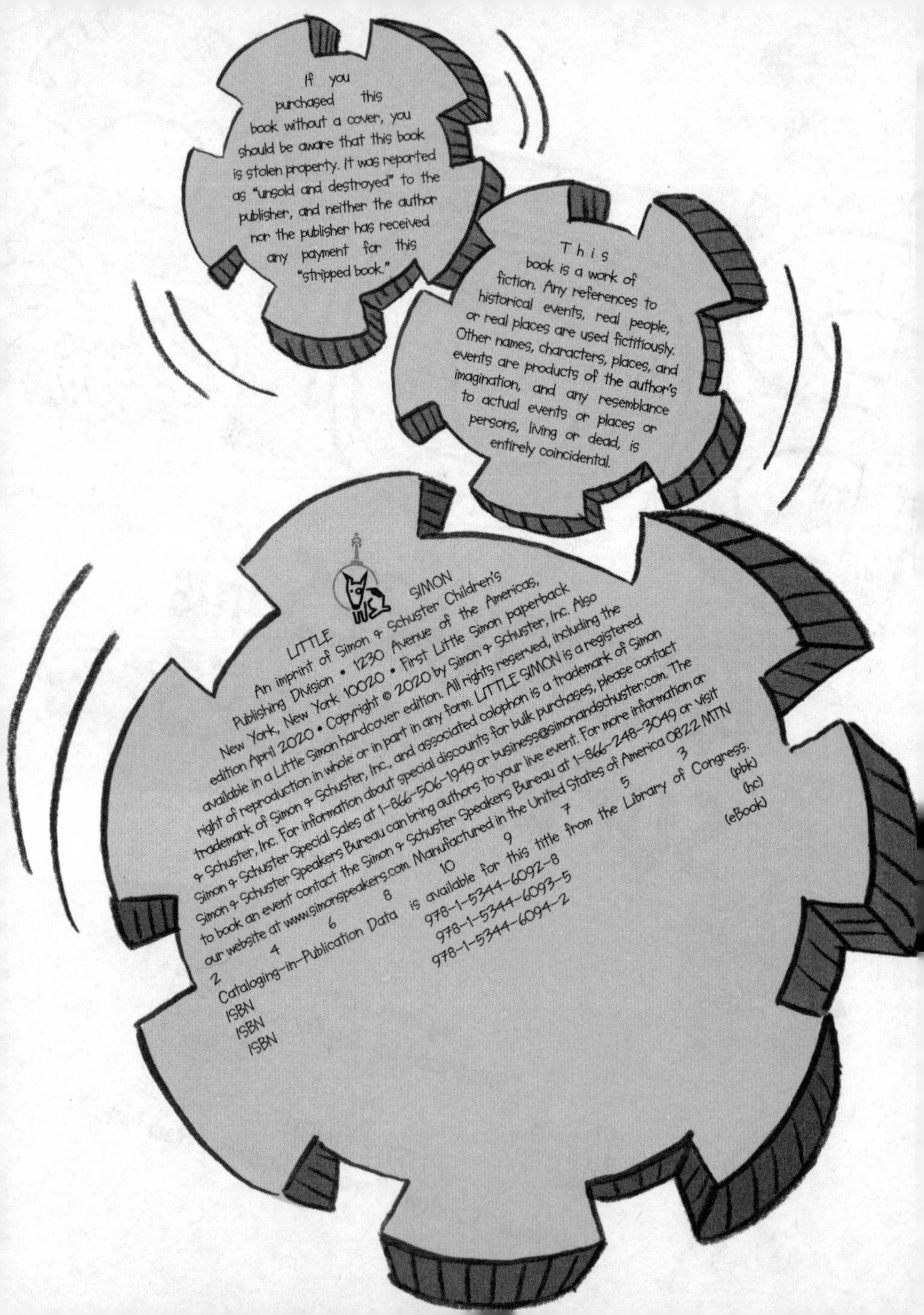

LITTLE SIMON
An imprint of Simon & Schuster Children's Publishing Division • 1230 Avenue of the Americas, New York, New York 10020 • First Little Simon paperback edition April 2020 Also available in a Little Simon hardcover edition. For information about special discounts for bulk purchases, please contact Simon & Schuster Special Sales at 1-866-506-1949 or business@simonandschuster.com. The Simon & Schuster Speakers Bureau can bring authors to your live event. For more information or to book an event contact the Simon & Schuster Speakers Bureau at 1-866-248-3049 or visit our website at www.simonspeakers.com. Manufactured in the United States of America 0822 MTN
2 4 6 8 10 9 7 5 3
Cataloging-in-Publication Data is available for this title from the Library of Congress.
ISBN 978-1-5344-6092-8 (pbk)
ISBN 978-1-5344-6093-5 (hc)
ISBN 978-1-5344-6094-2 (eBook)

CONTENTS

CHAPTER 1

A Normal Day

Hello, humans! It's another normal day in Botsburg. The bird-bots are chirping.

Grown-up Bots are working.

And the student Bots are learning at school.
BOT SCHOOL
ZZZZZZ
Wait! It looks like some students have escaped!

BUS
STUDENTS! PLEASE DON'T RUN. I KNOW YOU ARE VERY EXCITED ABOUT OUR FIELD TRIP TODAY.
Phew. They are not escaping. They are getting on the school bus.

EXIT
LITTLE ROBOTS
ALCOTT-BOT
SUPER BOT
TIME TO MAKE SURE ALL MY STUDENTS ARE HERE. HEAD COUNT SCAN ENGAGE.

What are you two buckets of bolts reading?
It's the latest issue of Super Bot!
LITTLE ROBOTS
SUPER BOT
SB

YOU'LL NEVER GET AWAY WITH THIS.
HA, HA, HA! IT'S OVER, SUPER BOT.

Comic books?! Ugh, comic books are BORING.
No, Tinny! This issue is great. See, Super Bot is in trouble!
Her archenemy, Super Bad Brad, has her trapped!
LITTLE ROBOTS
SUPER BOT

THE ONLY WAY TO STOP THE DOOMSDAY DEVICE IS BY PRESSING THE BUTTON WAY OVER THERE. AND YOU ARE WAY OVER HERE!
STOP
DO NOT PRESS!

THE WORLD WOULD BE IN TROUBLE...
IF I DIDN'T HAVE SUPER STRETCH ARMS!
WAVE!

LOOKS LIKE I KNOW HOW TO PUSH YOUR BUTTONS, SUPER BAD BRAD.
SB
TOUPEE SNATCH!
ANNOYING POKE!

That...

That...

was...

was...

so cool!

so NOT cool!

I wish we could be superheroes.
But you're already super zeroes to me.
Aw, thanks, Tinny.

No, wait, that wasn't a compliment. I wasn't being nice to you!

Not many superheroes were created on field trips. Hmm, I wonder where the Bots are going today?
BUS
Radioactive Spider Petting Zoo?

BUS
Gamma Rays R Us?

BUS
Super Toxic Science Lab?

NOT A SECRET HIDEOUT
BUS
The Bot Cave?

BUS
Magical Rings and Things?

FOODY FOODS
SALE!
BUS
The Supermarket?

HERE WE ARE, CLASS. THE GIANT SPEAKER FACTORY!
BUS

GIANT
SPEAKER
FACTORY

CHAPTER 2 Radio Active

Welcome to the wild world of speakers. Speakers make sound.

You may ask, "What kinds of sounds do speakers make?" They make sounds like...

Alarm clocks.
BEEP! BEEP!
BEEP!

Fire drills.
CLANG! CLANG! CLANG!

Mosquitoes with microphones.
BZZZZ! BZZZZ!
Loud eaters with microphones.
SMACK! SMACK!

Car alarms.
EE-OO-EE-OO! WHOOP WHOOP! AOOGA AOOGA!

Oh, and Bots scratching chalkboards with microphones.
SCREEEEEEEEEECHHHH!

What do these speakers do?

Those speakers are off-limits!
Please don't touch them.
They are so loud that music played through them would be heard all around the universe.
Oh, really?
ON
BUTTON

ON
BUTTON

The music was so loud, other planets could probably hear it.

It even reached planet Earth!

But what would a radio-active sound wave that strong do to a normal Bot?

CHAPTER 3

Super Sonic

This is a good song.

But the sound is crushing us!

My bolts are going to burst!
What?
I said my bolts are going to burst!
Your butts are going to burp?

My BOLTS are going to...never mind, just look!

Rob! Your bolts are going to burst!

I'll save you! Up, up, blast away!

ROB! ARE YOU ALL RIGHT?
I'm okay. I feel good. Actually, I feel better than good. I feel great.

I feel great, too.
Wow! Joe! You're flying! That can only mean one thing...

WE ARE SUPER

HEROES!

CHAPTER 4

Costumes

WAIT! THEY MAY BE SUPERHEROES, BUT THEY ARE STILL MY STUDENTS!
Your students will be fine, ma'am.
This is, um, part of the tour.
But we do have a few more forms for you to fill out.

Here we are! The costume room!
COSTUME ROOM
Why do we need a costume room?

Because superheroes need...

costumes!

Now it's time for a superhero fashion show!

Catman?
Ice-Cream Man?
Arrgman?
Snowman?
Clownman?
Clownman?

Unicornman?
Hydrantman?
Robman?

Mastermind?
Puppyboy?
Joeman?

Hmm, obviously you don't know what superhero costumes look like. Why don't you try these?

These suits fit perfectly!

WRONG! Switch the costumes, Bots!

TA

DA!

CHAPTER 5

Super Powers?

I know! You can fly! And I can... I can...
Hmm, what can I do?
Maybe you have...*lightning-fast* *reflexes!* CATCH THIS WATER BALLOON!

Hmm, you don't have lightning-fast reflexes, but you are water-resistant!

Don't worry, Rob! I'll dry you!

More like "I'll *fry* you."

That radio-active speaker must have given you some kind of superpower.
We just need to find it.
SUPER STRENGTH
No.
SQUISH!
SUPER SPEED
Um...
Um, no.
WALL CRAWLING
JUMP!
No.
FWUMP!

FLYING
JUMP
Nope.
CLUNK.
INVISIBILITY
Nah.
LASER EYEBALL
No, that's just a flashlight eyeball.
SCORPION TAIL!
I don't have a tail.

I can stretch my arms.
That works!

BLAR!
BLAR!
What's that?
Oh, goody! That's the MEANWHILE alarm! It means that while we've been finding your superpowers, something bad has happened in Botsburg! To the MEANWHILE Machine!
BLAR!
BLAR!

CHAPTER 6

Meanwhile

Well, when something happens here, we experience it. But that doesn't mean that things stop happening everywhere else in the world.
For example, you have been becoming superheroes here.
MEANWHILE, in another part of the universe...
MEANWHILE
ELLIPSES!
3RD PERSON NARRATION!

The students continued their tour.

An ice-cream spaceship got stuck before it reached the playground.

The Dragon Bots were watching a play.

The Oozy Goozers moved to the perfect planet.

Shhh, someone is hard at work.

But these are the Bots we should worry about. Watch.

MEANWHILE...

POWER
XOXO
HOW ARE WE GONNA ESCAPE, BOSS?
WE'RE GONNA USE THIS!

MEANWHILE...

WOW, A SUPERCOMPUTER! DID YOU HACK THE PRISON AND TAKE CONTROL OVER EVERYTHING? ARE YOU GOING TO USE IT TO OPEN ALL THE JAIL CELLS AND TRAP ALL THE GUARDS?
011

YEAH! AND THEN, ARE YOU GONNA USE IT TO HACK THE CITY SO WE CAN STEAL ANYTHING WE WANT WITHOUT GETTING CAUGHT? IF SO, CAN WE HIT THE MUSEUM FIRST? I JUST LOVE THAT MONOCHROME LISA PAINTING.

POWER
HUH? NO, YOU RUSTED BOLTS! LOOK *BEHIND* THE COMPUTER.

MEANWHILE...

POWER
SEE? I'VE BEEN USING THIS TINY SPOON TO DIG AN ESCAPE HOLE IN THE WALL! THEN I HID IT BEHIND A SUPERCOMPUTER, WHERE THE GUARDS WOULD NEVER FIND IT.
YOU'RE SO SMART, BOSS!
BUT WE COULD HAVE USED THE SUPERCOMPUTER TO TAKE OVER ALL OF BOTSBURG!
111

MEANWHILE...

I DON'T WANT TO TAKE OVER ALL OF BOTSBURG.
I WANT TO ESCAPE, THEN I WANT TO TAKE OVER ALL OF BOTSBURG.
0001
BUT... BUT... BUT...
011

POWER
HEY, JUST BECAUSE WE ARE BAD BOTS DOESN'T MEAN WE SAY BAD WORDS.
OH, YOU ARE GOING TO BE IN SO MUCH TROUBLE WHEN I TELL THE GUARDS WHAT YOU SAID!
111

MEANWHILE...

AND YOU DON'T WANT TO GET IN TROUBLE JUST AS WE ARE ABOUT TO ESCAPE. SO STICK TO THE PLAN.
YEAH, BOSS. OKAY. TAKE IT EASY OR YOU'LL RUN OUT OF BATTERIES.

POWER
CARE TO TELL US THE REST OF THE PLAN?
NO, I DON'T. IF YOU WANT TO KNOW MORE, JUMP IN THE HOLE AND FIND OUT.
0001
011

MEANWHILE...
It looks like Super Joe and Stretchy Rob have their first adventure!
IT'S NOT A DOT DOT DOT!
3RD PERSON NARRATION!

Stretchy Rob? Do I have to keep that name? It's not very cool.

CHAPTER 7

Super Bad Bots

POWER

WHERE TO NOW, BOSS?

011

OH, CAN WE GO TAKE A DANCE OR ART CLASS? I KNOW I'M A BAD BOT, BUT I'VE ALWAYS WANTED TO BE AN ARTIST.

MEANWHILE...

NO ART CLASS. WE NEED TO PAINT A BIGGER PICTURE. ONE THAT BOTSBURG WILL NEVER FORGET.
POP!
0001

WANTED
0001
011
111
YOU MEAN LIKE A BILLBOARD SIGN?

POW
NO! WE'RE HEADING TO THE ONE PLACE NO ONE WILL THINK TO LOOK FOR A GROUP OF BAD BOTS. WE'RE HEADING TO THE GIANT SPEAKER FACTORY!
RUB!
RUB!
RUB!
?
?
111
011

MEANWHILE...

THE SPEAKER FACTORY...
BUS

FACTORY
HAS A SUPER-COMPUTER...

WE CAN USE TO TAKE OVER BOTSBURG!

POWER
AND HERE IT IS!
UM, ISN'T THIS THE SAME SUPER-COMPUTER THAT WE HAD IN JAIL?

MEANWHILE...
1000

POWER
NO! IT'S DIFFERENT BECAUSE *THIS* SUPERCOMPUTER DOESN'T HAVE AN ESCAPE HOLE BEHIND IT!
I'm beginnin
to like th
Bot.

And this supercomputer is protected by SUPERHEROES!

WHAT?
WHAT?
WHAT?
More like SUPER ZEROES.

Get ready...
for a super party!

WHAT?
0001

WHAT?
011

OH, I LOVE PARTIES!

Even their catchphrases are dumb.

It's busting Bad Bot time!
Let's do this!

WHOOSH!

WHAT ARE THEY DOING?
0001
WIGGLE!

THAT BOT IS FLYING IN CIRCLES. AND THAT BOT IS WIGGLING HIS ARMS.
IT'S A DANCE PARTY!
And dance parties need music!
DON'T PUSH!

0001
R

Now we have Superheroes AND Super Bad Bots!
DON'T PUSH!

CHAPTER 8
Mastermind!
WHAT ARE YOU DOING?
I AM MAKING MY DREAMS COME TRUE!
JUMP!

All my life, I've loved comic books.
THE DARK BOT!
SUPER BOT!
IRON BOT!
DARE-BOT!

But the real world was so boring!

So I built these super speakers to make superheroes.

And super villains!

NOW THE WORLD IS MY COMIC BOOK! AND I AM THE MASTERMIND!

It's up to us to stop this, Rob. We're the superheroes.
Right! First we need to stop this music.

Got it!
Super stretchy arms, away!

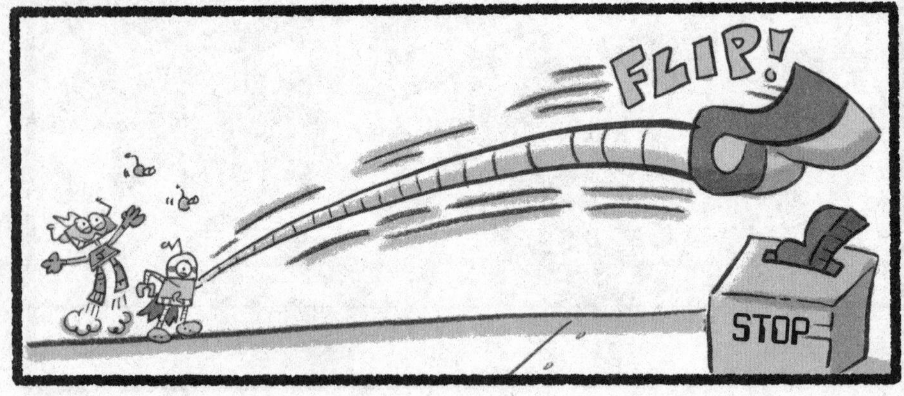
FLIP!
STOP

Whoa! That was so cool!

Now we need to stop the Bad Bots!

YOU MEAN, THE SUPER BAD BOTS!
BB

LET'S DANCE.
HOW DID YOU GET NEW COSTUMES? AND ARE ANYONE ELSE'S EARS RINGING?
011

I'll take the dancer. You handle the Bad Bot Boss.
Okay, wait, what?!

Time to boogie!
SECRET HEADPHONES!

OH, I LOVE THIS SONG! IT MAKES ME WANT TO DANCE FOREVER!

One Bad
Bot down! Two
to go!

DON'T JUST STAND THERE! GET RID OF THOSE SUPERHEROES SO WE CAN TAKE OVER THE CITY!
WHAT? I CAN'T HEAR YOU. THE RINGING IN MY EARS IS TOO LOUD!
RING!
BB
011

I SAID, GO FIGHT!
GOOD NIGHT? IS IT DARK OUT ALREADY?

WHAT?! LOOK AT THE SUNLIGHT OUTSIDE!
RUN RIGHT OUTSIDE?
SEEMS WEIRD, BUT YOU'RE THE BOSS!

ONCE AGAIN, I HAVE TO DO EVERYTHING MYSELF.
PREPARE TO RUST IN PEACE, SUPER ZEROES.
ROLL!
ROLL!

CHAPTER 9

KA-POW!

Oh, our superhero Bots are in trouble now! I am almost too scared to watch what happens.

Almost.

Rob, I just realized something. I've always been able to fly. I have rockets for legs.
Oh yeah. And I've always been able to stretch my arms.
Does that mean we're...
NOT SUPER?!

Um, hi, Mr. Super Bad Bot Boss. It turns out that we aren't actually super, so you win.
Yeah, that was a fun game. Thanks for playing!

NO, NO, NO! YOU CAN'T QUIT BECAUSE YOU'RE NORMAL. YOU TRIED TO STOP ME FROM TAKING OVER THE CITY, AND NOW YOU'RE GOING TO PAY!
BB

GET BACK HERE!
START!
POWER FADING... NEED POWER PELLET. HERE'S ONE.
Um, that's not a power pellet.

SLOWING DOWN...
BATTERY RUNNING LOW...
END!

KA-POWERING DOWN!!!
WE DID IT!
BB
J

JOE! ROB! I DON'T KNOW WHAT YOU DID, BUT IT'S TIME TO HEAD BACK TO SCHOOL. LET'S GET OUT OF HERE BEFORE ANYTHING REALLY WEIRD HAPPENS.

CHAPTER 10

Super Friends

Back on the bus, Joe and Rob realized that they didn't need to be super to have great adventures.

Because we really pushed his buttons!
Ha, ha, ha! That's a really bad joke!
TICKLE!
They just needed to have super friends.

TINNY &
Only!!!

HMM, WE ARE SHORT BY ONE STUDENT.
HAS ANYONE SEEN TINNY?

MEANWHILE...

Now it's time to take over Botsburg!

PLEASE ENTER PASSWORD:
CYBORG
TAP TAP

CYBORG
CYCLOPS
TAP TAP

CYBORG
CYCLOPS
SUPER HERO
TAP TAP

CYBORG
CYCLOPS
SUPER HERO
SUPER VILLAIN
TAP TAP TAP

CYBORG
CYCLOPS
SUPER HERO
SUPER VILLAIN

POWER

~~CYBORG~~
~~CYCLOPS~~
~~SUPER HERO~~
~~SUPER VILLAIN~~
Aw, I give up.

~~CYBORG~~
~~CYCLOPS~~
~~SUPER HERO~~
~~SUPER VILLAIN~~
JOE AND
There will be other chances to destroy Joe and Rob.

~~CYBORG~~
~~CYCLOPS~~
~~SUPER HERO~~
~~SUPER VILLAIN~~
JOE AND ROB

~~CYBORG~~
~~CYCLOPS~~
~~SUPER HERO~~
~~SUPER VILLAIN~~
JOE AND ROB
Password accepted.

TUNE IN NEXT TIME FOR...